The boy who likes to Spin

NEURODIVERSITY IN AN AUTISTIC CHILD

Written by Joahnes Gatdula

Illustrated by Cindy Mettana &
Lael Drew P Dela Cruz

I dedicate this book to my parents, family, and friends who have given me so much love and support. To all my students at The Child's World AGC, thank you for teaching me the value of humility and perseverance. To all of their parents, guardians, teachers and nannies, thank you for your love and patience. Lastly, to all SPED teachers, aides, therapists, and doctors. Thank you for your hard work serving our clients, students, and patients. – J.G.

I want to dedicate and thank my Mom and my little sister for the everlasting love and to the rest of my family who always support me. Most of all I want to thank my creator, God the father who gave me this wonderful life and talent.
And of course not to forget the author of the book my uncle, who believes in my capabilities. I heard lots of stories about his goodwill and how he achieved his goal. May you always be blessed to and continue to be a blessing to everyone. – LD

Hi! My name is Lucas.

I'm a non-verbal Autistic boy.

My world is different from yours.

Let me take you in it.

I live in this enchanting twirling

home filled with yellow trees that

makes me happy and excited.

I love to **spin** all day long. It makes me **feel good**, like I'm on a never-ending carousel ride!

I also like to flicker my fingers whenever I'm excited or anxious. It's like looking at the rays of stars that glimmer in the lovely skylight.

Sometimes, I feel like to be alone, I want to play in a corner. It feels like walking in the parted ocean, where the fishes and corals can't bother me anymore.

I also like to clap, hop and squeeze myself. It feels **calming and relaxing** at the same time.

It's like a light rain and lightning during a storm.

One day, someone took my favorite toy out of my hand. It seemed that I got lost in the woods, **alone and afraid**, then I saw this big bad wolf with my teddy bear in his mouth.

As I lay there, I cried and felt the tears stream down my face. I imagined it was raining hard with all the thunderstorms and lightning.

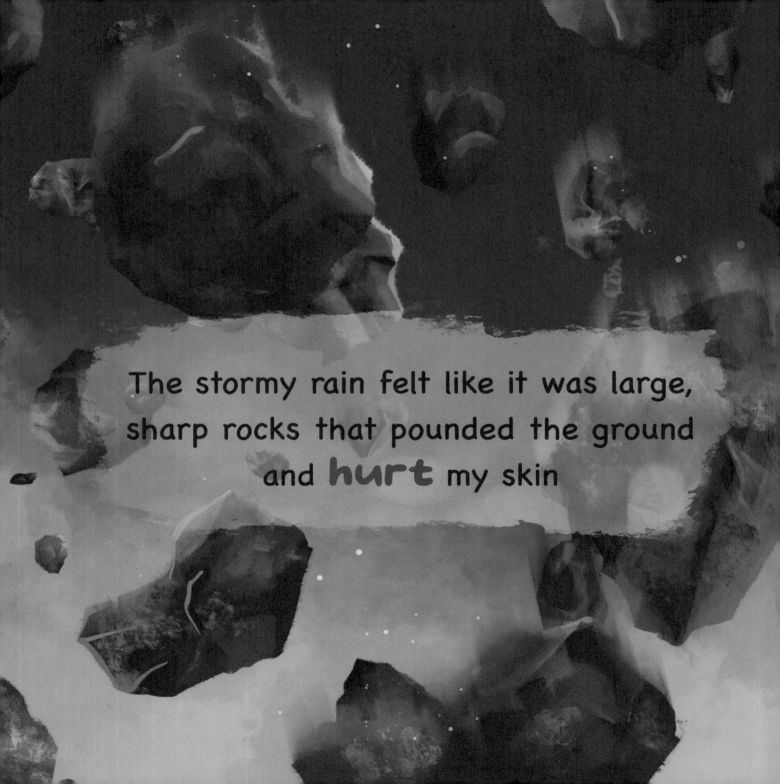

The stormy rain felt like it was large, sharp rocks that pounded the ground and **hurt** my skin

I imagined **running** through the woods, trying to escape the pelting rain, but I took a thorny bush and a jagged rock with every step.

It was my mother, who had been searching for me all day. She hugged me and took me back home.

Sometimes,
I feel like my mother is tired.
I tried to look into her eyes.
I want to thank her for all her
sacrifices in caring for me.

I love my mother. She takes care of me. Although, I cannot speak, I try to **touch** her face when I can. I hope she knows that I **love** her so much.

If only I could **Say** how much I love my parents. I will draw and paint the world with all the colors I can.

Here are some references for Autism, Neurodiversity, Occupational Therapy and Sensory Integration:

https://my.clevelandclinic.org/health/symptoms/23154-neurodivergent

https://www.health.harvard.edu/blog/what-is-neurodiversity-202111232645

https://exceptionalindividuals.com/neurodiversity/

https://www.aota.org/-/media/corporate/files/aboutot/professionals/whatisot/cy/fact-sheets/factsheet_sensoryintegration.pdf

https://www.autismcrc.com.au/access/supporting-children

https://www.facebook.com/tcwagc1982/

Printed in Great Britain
by Amazon